For Anaé and Jean.
Matthieu

For Flavie and her imaginary friends.
Michaël

This edition first published in 2012 by Gecko Press
PO Box 9335, Marion Square, Wellington 6141, New Zealand
info@geckopress.com

English language edition © Gecko Press Ltd 2012

Original title: Un mammouth dans le frigo
Text by Michaël Escoffier and illustrations by Matthieu Maudet
© 2011 l'école des loisirs, Paris
Translation © Gecko Press 2012

A catalogue record for this book is available from the National Library of New Zealand.

Translated by Linda Burgess
Typesetting by Luke Kelly, New Zealand
Printed by Everbest, China

ISBN hardback: 978-1-877579-14-1
ISBN paperback: 978-1-877579-15-8

For more curiously good books, visit www.geckopress.com

A Mammoth in the Fridge

by Michaël Escoffier
and illustrated by Matthieu Maudet

GECKO PRESS

'Dad! Dad!
There's a mammoth in the fridge!'

'Don't be silly, Noah.
Come and eat your chips.'

'Dad! It's true! Look!'
'Aaaah! Keep away, son. It might bite.'

'Sweetheart – call the fire brigade.'

Wheee-ooo! Wheee-ooo! Wheee-ooo! Wheee-ooo! Wheee-ooo! Wheee-ooo!

Wheee-ooo! Wheee-ooo! Wheee-ooo! Wheee-ooo! Wheee-ooo! Wheee-ooo!

'Morning, ma'am. We're here about the mammoth.'
'Oh, do come in...'

'Three!'

'Whooooops!'

'Catch it!
Quickly!'

Clip! Clop!

'Well, what now?'
'Be patient. It'll have to come down eventually.'

'Huh! We could be here till autumn.'

'Sorry, guys. We've got to go.'

'Come on. It's not our problem.'

'Look at these yummy carrots.'

'Come on...'

'Up you come. That's it!'

'Ssshh! Don't wake Mum and Dad.'

'I'm warning you – this is the last time I'll save you.
You'll get us all in trouble with your silly nonsense...'